Beyond The Laces

Written by
Bob Salomon and Rick Young

Illustrated by
Ken Jones

Stay Strong!
Love,
Santa

The book has been a group endeavor that could not have been accomplished without the efforts from many amazing people.
A sincere thanks to those who went "beyond:" Rick Young,
Ken Jones, Matthew Gallaro, Joe Cifelli, Tom Brisco, Randolf Knapp,
Lou Pucci and Marla McKenna.

A special thanks to my wife and two children. I am very grateful for the family God has given me. Without their foundation of love and support, Beyond The Laces would never have come to be.

It is also an honor to have this opportunity to help inspire youth through our storyline and movement that has the support of so many in the sports world. It is truly humbling, and a true blessing. Sincerely grateful.

– Bob Salomon

To my wife, Linda, and our children and grandchildren,
always an inspiration;
and especially to my grandmother,
Violet May Tribull,
who instilled in me a love of reading and, thus, writing.

– Rick Young

Cool, crisp, autumn winds,
where colored leaves swirl 'round,
rainbow reds, and yellows too,
fill the air of our town.

But it's not just leaves a-fallin',
upon the air so free;
for footballs fly on autumn winds,
"Hut-one, hut-two, hut-three."

Yet, not all who long for football
are included in the play.
Some only watch from sidelines,
just waiting for that day.

When they too will get a chance,
making it more than just their dream
to catch the winning touchdown pass,
and be a member of the team.

"Hey Son, whatcha doing?"
came his father's startling call.
"Nothing Dad," with lowered head,
"just watching kids play ball."

His father changed the subject,
to help lessen the pain.
"Tomorrow, Son, is Sunday.
Do you think they'll win the game?"

Then Mom is at the doorway.
"Hey, is everything okay?"
"Sure, Mom," the boy replies,
"we're just talking about football day."

But Mom's eyes seem saddened,
her own heart feeling brittle.
"I'm fine, Mom," the boy goes on,
"I'm tired, well, just a little."

"How's he really doing?"
Mom asks in whispered tone.
She looks in her husband's eyes,
"He often seems so alone."

Her husband nods in silence,
on this subject they don't dwell,
"You know what the doctor said,
he has to want to get well."

Next day, football Sunday!
A game filled with yells and cheers;
Father and Son at the TV set,
cherished moments and forgotten tears.

"Can they pull this out? I hope they do!
An upset win would be heaven!"
Pounding hearts, on edge of their seats,
"It's all up to our 87!"

Yet now the boy is growing tired;
he can take the strain no more;
heavy limbs, and heavy eyes,
no longer focused on the score.

"Dad, can I lie beside you?
I tried my best to watch the game;
but I'm so very weary,
I'm just not feeling all the same."

Quiet feet walk down the hallway,
without a sound Dad climbs the stairs.
The light load in his arms is nothing,
compared to a father's cares.

With a loving kiss upon his forehead,
the boy is tucked in bed.
"Tomorrow's a long day, my son.
Sweet dreams," his father said.

Offered there in the hallway,
a father's request at length,
"Please, lead and guide us,
our prayer is to have strength."

Next morning in the doctor's office,
the son's exam well underway,
"Did you see that win?" his doctor asked.
"Your 87 sure saved the day!"
"No," said the boy when examined,
expert fingers searching for cures.
"But I saw the replay this morning,
with comments just like yours!"

"Well," continued the doctor,
"I am going to make you healthy and fit.
Together we'll share in a victory;
like 87, we'll never give up or quit."

Out in the hallway, through hospital bustle,
the doctor with the parents alone.
Showing them charts and medical records,
all truths were now clearly shown.

"I'm telling you that he can be healed;
there's no room for a Doubting Thomas.
We'll see that he's made better again,
this is my own solemn promise.
His condition we know is medically sound,
which, frankly, is nothing new;
to be finally healed of this hurtful disease,
is something he must want to do!"

Days later at home in the kitchen,
they discuss the doctor's clear view.
"We must find a way to uplift him,
a way to help him get through."

"What if we wrote to his favorite player?
87 just might do the trick."

"I'm not sure that he'd even take notice;
would he even care… that our boy is so sick?"

That night Dad stirred at the table,
breaking pencil points on to his pad.
"A million to one," he mumbled so softly.
"But I must try…I am his dad."

In a parent's heart there is always the hope,
and any idea is worth a try.
We never give up, we only give more,
there's no time for the asking, "Why?"

The football player, dedicated and true,
an inspiration on gridiron green;
greeted by all as a present day hero,
to believe, in person he must be seen.

With muscles and brawn and fearsome position,
each player must do his part.
Yet, under the jerseys, the mud-stained jerseys,
lies a child of a man's beating heart.

A few weeks later; a Wednesday, yes,
the day of Thanksgiving Eve,
Dad gets the mail, opens a letter, and yells,
"This you'll never believe!"

Mom hurries to read over his shoulder,
a mother's joy now on her face,
"Do you think he will be so able?"
Yet this moment she wants to embrace.

As Mom and Dad sit side-by-side,
a hush hangs in the air.
They realize in that moment of silence,
they hold the answer to their prayer.

Then comes the big day, cold, yet sunny,
the stadium filled with the crowd,
the family walks to front-row seating;
they can't believe they are allowed!

They shuffle to seats, fans aplenty.
All of them making a fuss.
Dad says to one, "These seats are amazing.
I can't believe he gave them to us!"
The woman responds with a smile,
as Dad continues to say,
"My son is not well; we are so thankful.
His favorite, 87, sure made this day!"

The woman continues to smile,
as if she already knew.
She settles the girls at her side and replied,
"You know, he's our favorite too!"

"We just wish the world knew the real 87,
after all, he's worth so much more.
He is caring inside; a true winner inside.
No matter the game's final score."

W histles blew; they battled quarter to quarter.
The crowd always shouting for more.
As the clock ticked down to the final seconds,
the truth remained in the score.

Down by five points, with one play remaining,
every fan on the edge of their seat.
The boy knew that without a touchdown
his team would go down in defeat.

And then the last play, as if in slow motion,
the pass hung high in the air.
With outstretched arms, and desperate fingers…
87's hands were suddenly there!

The stadium then simply erupted,
from fans came shouts of joy.
The loudest of all from front row seating,
with a newfound voice from the boy!

"He did it! He did it! And I saw it in person!
Oh Mom and Dad, it was great as can be!"
His parents could cry at the sight of their son,
cheering with a heart now carefree!

Outside the park, hoping to glimpse 87,
against the crowd's exiting tide,
they spied the woman who sat beside them,
with her two girls walking along by her side.

And there in the line of players,
just as the boy always hoped to see,
was 87, the touchdown hero,
walking with them…his own family!

Then with a glance the woman whispered,
and toward the boy 87 had a clear view;
the child's eyes grew wide, his heart skipped a beat.
Could this moment really be true?

With a hand on his shoulder
87 looked down at the boy.
"Son, you are special; don't quit, just get better.
When you do, it will bring me great joy."

And with a smile, that winning-catch smile,
a game ball was silently passed along.
The boy hardly breathing whispered a "Thank You."
And he knew that he really belonged!

From the window the truth is clearly before them;
their feelings, no words can explain.
For parents whose joy can hardly be spoken,
to have the child they love back in the game!

ONE YEAR LATER...

To quit is to lose; you cannot give up.
You simply can never give in.
Just turn your back on those nagging doubts
and fears that you may never win.

"It's not just football; it's a lesson in life."
The boy would listen as his father would say.
"It's beyond the game; it's beyond the laces.
It's courage as you face each new day."

And the boy knew, yes he had to agree,
for success all it took to achieve
was a gift that came from Number 87:
the desire and will to believe.

INSPIRING CHILDREN THROUGH KINDNESS
UNITING TO MAKE A DIFFERENCE

My journey started years ago when I felt a desire to use sports as a means to help children. I put together a team of dedicated people who shared that same vision. As a result, Danjulie, LLC, was established in order to "Inspire Children Through Kindness." We have done this by taking on projects that make a difference in the lives of our youth. Danjulie's efforts have been supported by a growing list of well-known professional athletes and related corporate organizations which have assisted in aiding children. Funds have been raised through books sales, events, and programs that have gone directly to organizations helping children, and more importantly changing lives and making a difference. Through kindness we show that people do care.

Grateful,
Bob Salomon

Please visit: www.BeyondTheLaces.com
To get involved contact Bob: ContactUs@BeyondTheLaces.com

Beyond the storyline of our book is a deeper meaning:
We are eager to inspire through kindness by assisting the development of America's next generation.
To do this, we are harnessing the influence and star power of the professional athlete, which will unite all sports to impact the lives of children and families.
The Beyond The Laces team plans to tour with various sports figures visiting hospitals, schools, and youth programs around the country to showcase the story's message of never giving up.

"To quit is to lose; you cannot give up.
You simply can never give in.
Just turn your back on those nagging doubts
and fears that you may never win."

- Beyond The Laces
www.BeyondTheLaces.com